OLIVIA™
A Sweet Surprise for Mom

By Farrah McDoogle
Illustrated by Jared Osterhold

Simon Spotlight
New York   London   Toronto   Sydney   New Delhi

Based on the TV series OLIVIA™ as seen on Nickelodeon™

SIMON SPOTLIGHT
An imprint of Simon & Schuster Children's Publishing Division
1230 Avenue of the Americas, New York, New York 10020
This Simon Spotlight paperback edition March 2015
OLIVIA™ Ian Falconer Ink Unlimited, Inc. and © 2015 Ian Falconer and Classic Media, LLC
For information about special discounts for bulk purchases, please contact
Simon & Schuster Special Sales at 1-866-506-1949 or business@simonandschuster.com.
Manufactured in the United States of America 0215 LAK
1 2 3 4 5 6 7 8 9 10
ISBN 978-1-4814-2763-0
ISBN 978-1-4814-2764-7 (eBook)

Olivia was snuggled in bed listening to a story. She loved bedtime stories, but tonight there was one little problem. . . .

"Psst, Mom . . . do you want me to take it from here?" Olivia asked.

"Hmm, what?" Olivia's mom's eyes flew open. "I'm sorry, honey. I'm extra tired tonight and I guess I dozed off."

Olivia told her mom not to worry—she could finish the story.

After her mother left her room, Olivia finished the story by herself. But then she lay awake thinking for a little while. Her mom was tired because she worked so hard, Olivia decided. She deserved a special surprise to say thank you for everything she did.

Just before she fell asleep, Olivia came up with a plan.

"So you see, Dad, that's why I need you to take me to the grocery store," Olivia said the next morning.

"I think a special surprise breakfast is a great idea," her dad replied, "but you should keep in mind that your mom really enjoys having cereal for breakfast."

"Cereal isn't very special," Olivia insisted. "Especially the kind Mom likes. It's not even sweet!"

At the grocery store, Olivia shopped carefully. Finally every item was crossed off her list.

"Don't forget to buy some cereal," her dad reminded her.

Olivia didn't think she would need cereal. But she put a box in the cart anyway, just in case.

The next morning Olivia woke up early and tiptoed downstairs. When she got to the kitchen she was surprised to find . . .

. . . her mom was already in the kitchen, eating a bowl of cereal!
"What are you doing up so early?" Olivia asked.
"I have an early meeting with a client," her mother explained.
Olivia vowed to wake up extra early the next day.

The next morning Olivia woke up so early that it was still dark outside. She tiptoed downstairs. When she got to the kitchen she was surprised to find . . .

. . . her dad, Ian, and Baby William were awake and waiting for her.

"What are you doing up so early?" Olivia asked.

"We woke up to help you," her father explained.

"Thanks, but I have this all planned out," Olivia told them. "You can go back to sleep."

"But Olivia," said Ian, "I want to help with the special surprise!"

"You'll be glad we're here," her dad added. "We can help."

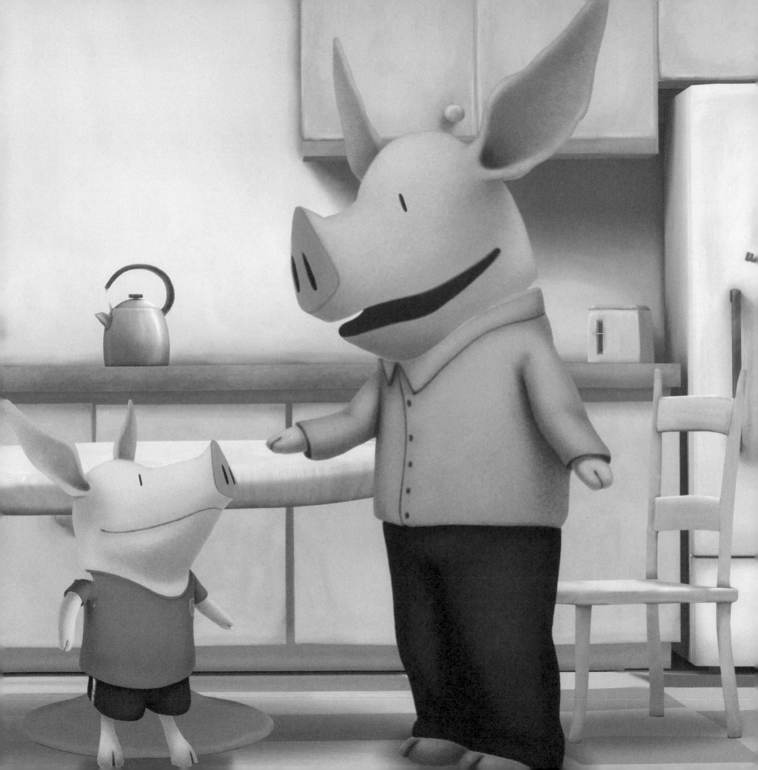

Having helpers wasn't part of Olivia's plan, but she decided to put them to work. "Dad, you can mix up the pancake batter. Ian, you can scramble the eggs. Baby William, you can sit there and draw a picture and not touch anything!"

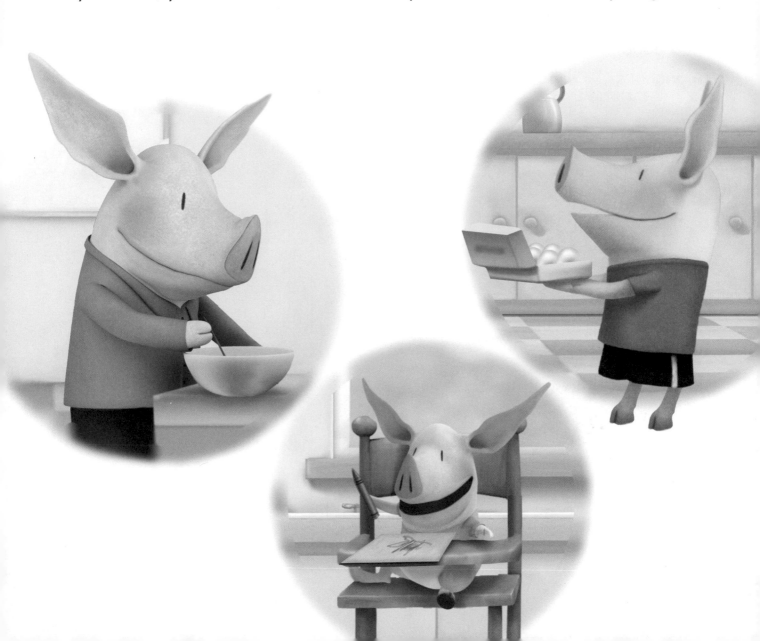

Things did not go according to Olivia's plan.
First Baby William knocked over the freshly
squeezed orange juice that Olivia had made.
Then Ian dropped half of the eggs on the floor.
"It's a good thing we still have more eggs and
the pancakes," Olivia said.

But then the doorbell rang. Dad turned away from the pancakes and slipped on the broken eggs. He bumped into Olivia, and then Olivia dropped the rest of the eggs on the floor.

"Ian, can you go answer the door while I clean this up?" Olivia asked.

"Whoever it is, please tell them to come back later!"

"It was Francine," Ian explained when he came back. "She was dropping off Gwendolyn because you agreed to take care of her while Francine's family goes out of town."

"That's right," Olivia said. "Just make sure to keep Gwendolyn—"

Just then an orange blur zipped through the kitchen, followed by a white blur.

"—away from Perry, because he likes to chase her," Olivia finished.

"I will go deal with that," said Father, running after Perry and Gwendolyn. Olivia continued to clean up the eggs from the floor. "At least we still have the pancakes," she said.

"Do you smell something burning?" Ian asked.

"Oh no! The pancakes!" Olivia cried. "What am I going to do now? We have no juice, no eggs, and no pancakes."

Olivia had an idea. She grabbed a bowl and poured some cereal into it. She put the bowl on a tray and looked at it. It didn't look very special.

"I want to help!" said Ian.

"Can you find some decorations for the tray to make it look special?" Olivia asked.

Ian took the picture Baby William had been coloring.
"How about this?" he asked.
Olivia took the picture and added a note: "Dear Mom,
we just wanted to say thank you to you for working so
hard. We love you!"

Together with Ian, her dad, and Baby William, Olivia brought the tray with the cereal and the picture upstairs to her mom.

"Thank you for doing this for me," Mother said with a sleepy smile. "I feel very special. This is the perfect surprise!"

Olivia gave her mom a big hug. "We worked all morning on it!"